Other books in this series

JONATHAN MARK AT GRANNY'S
JONATHAN MARK AT THE DOCTOR'S
JONATHAN MARK IN THE KITCHEN
JONATHAN MARK AT THE SEASIDE
JONATHAN MARK IN THE PARK

Other books by Jacqueline Sibley

STORY TIME TWO
STORY TIME FOUR

Made and printed in Great Britain by Purnell & Sons Ltd., Paulton (Somerset) & London
ISBN 0 279 85421 5 ·

Jacqueline Sibley

JONATHAN MARK AT HOME

Illustrated by
Walter Rieck

SCRIPTURE UNION   5 WIGMORE STREET   LONDON   WIH OAD

Jonathan Mark was
four. He lived in a
little white house
with his Mummy and
Daddy and his baby
sister, Catherine.

The little white house had a blue door and a bell that rang 'Ding dong' when anyone pressed it.

Jonathan Mark could just reach the door bell if he stood on his toes.

Every morning Mummy called,
'Jonathan Mark, it's time to get up.'
And Jonathan Mark would jump
out of bed thinking, 'I wonder what
I'll do today.'

After breakfast, Daddy always said a little prayer.

He said something like this, 'Please, God, take care of us today. Help us to do all the things we ought to do. Help us to be kind and helpful to the people we meet. Amen.'

Jonathan Mark said, 'Amen.'
Then he opened his eyes
and said, 'Daddy, does God really
hear us when we talk to Him?'
'Yes,' said Daddy, 'God
always hears us when we
talk to Him.'

Soon Daddy set off
for work.
'Goodbye, every-
body,' he called.
He hurried
down the road
and caught
the big
bus that
went to town.

Jonathan Mark fetched his train from the toy cupboard. It had a bright shiny engine and two yellow carriages.

'Where shall we go today?' thought
Jonathan Mark. 'I know, we'll go to
the seaside. Blow the whistle, Mr.
Guard, we're off!

Ch ch-ch, Ch ch-ch, Ch ch-ch.'

Jonathan Mark pulled his engine
round and round the chair-hills
and under the table-tunnel
until he came to the seaside.

'I wish I had someone to play with,' he said. 'Never mind,' said Mummy, 'when I've put Catherine to sleep you can help me.'

So Jonathan Mark did some dusting for
Mummy. He dusted the table-tunnel.
He dusted the chair-hills. He
dusted the books on the bottom book
shelves. He couldn't quite reach the ones
at the top.

'Why don't you play in
the garden for a little
while?' asked Mummy. 'All right,' said Jonathan
Mark. 'I think I'll play with my wheelbarrow.'
Soon Jonathan Mark came in again. 'I wish I
had someone to play with,' he said.

But Mummy was busy.
She said, 'I'm sorry,
Jonathan Mark. I can't
play with you just now.
If I do there won't be
any dinner, and that would
never do, would it?'
So Jonathan Mark
played on his own
until dinner time.

Before they began to eat their dinner Mummy said, 'Would you say "Thank You" to God for our food, Jonathan Mark?'

So Jonathan Mark said, 'Thank You, God, for our lovely dinner.'

Then he opened his eyes and said, 'Does God really hear me when I say "Thank You" to Him?'

'Yes,' said Mummy. 'God always hears you when you talk to Him.'

After dinner Mummy read a story to
Jonathan Mark.

Suddenly they heard the door bell
ring, 'Ding dong'.

It was Mrs. Lawson and her little girl, Elizabeth.

They lived across the road in the house with the green door and the green gate.

Elizabeth was four, just like Jonathan Mark. She smiled at him when Mummy opened the door.

Mrs. Lawson said to Mummy, 'Could Elizabeth possibly stay with you this afternoon? My tooth is aching and I really must go to the dentist.'

'Of course she can,' said Mummy. So Elizabeth took off her coat and Mummy put it on a hanger.

Then Elizabeth and Jonathan Mark played together. They played with the blue engine and yellow carriages.

They looked at some picture books.

They had a lovely time.

They were sitting by the fire and
drinking orange squash when Mrs. Lawson
came back. Her tooth wasn't aching any more.
'We've had a lovely time,' Elizabeth
and Jonathan Mark said together.

'Then another day you must play together
in our house,' said Mrs. Lawson.

Jonathan Mark knew he would like that.

When Daddy came home from the office, Jonathan Mark told him all about his games with Elizabeth.

'We must remember to thank God for giving you such a happy time,' said Daddy.

'Yes, God always hears me when I talk to Him, doesn't He?' said Jonathan Mark.

Before Jonathan Mark climbed into bed, he said, 'Thank You, God, for a happy day. Thank You for Mummy and Daddy and baby Catherine. Thank You, too, for my friend Elizabeth.'

Then he fell asleep. Soon it would be morning and once again he would think, 'I wonder what I'll do today?'